SECOND CHANCE WITH THE MOUNTAIN MAN

A STEAMY SMALL TOWN ROMANCE

KELSIE CALLOWAY

Kelsie
CALLOWAY
DARK, DIRTY, AND DANGEROUS ROMANCE

CONTENTS

1. Allison 1
2. Grant 13
3. Allison 25
4. Grant 37
5. Allison 49
6. Allison 57

Also By Kelsie Calloway 67
Have you left a review? 69
Get a free Kelsie Calloway book! 71

ALLISON

I step out of my car in Wildwood Ridge, my heels crunching on gravel. The air is thick with pine and nostalgia, wrapping around me like a familiar shawl frayed at the edges. It's been years since I've breathed this mountain air, but it feels like only yesterday.

"Still the same old Wildwood," I murmur to myself, though the words sound foreign in the vastness of open space. Mrs. O'Leary's apple pies scent the breeze, a recipe unchanged by time, pulling me back into a world where every corner holds a memory.

As I walk towards my childhood home, each step feels heavy, reluctant. I can almost hear the creak of the gate that no longer swings on its hinges. My fingers trace the peeling paint of the picket fence, the white now giving way to the gray of weathered wood and lost time.

"He kept mom's roses," I whisper. They're wild now, a riotous explosion of color unchecked and untamed —so different from the neatly pruned bushes she tended with such care when she was alive. But now they're both gone, leaving me with the house and a thousand faded memories.

I let out a breath I didn't realize I was holding and lean against the fence, my gaze sweeping over the house. "You've aged, old friend," I say softly, allowing the corners of my lips to lift in a bitter-sweet smile.

The house is larger than when I left. My father was always building onto it; he called it his never-ending project. My heart clenches, missing his reassuring presence.

It's been ten long years since I left Wildwood Ridge. I said goodbye to my family, my childood, and my first love.

"Grant," I say his name aloud, testing it on my tongue, wondering if he still remembers me as vividly as I do him. "I bet you never left." My voice is a mix of admiration and accusation, for he always had roots here deeper than the pines that tower above.

I steel myself to push past the gate, to reclaim a fragment of the life I left behind. This wild, untamed garden is just the beginning. Beyond it lies a house full of echoes, an echo of love, loss, and the chance to find redemption in the clearing of overgrown paths.

The door creaks on ancient hinges, a sound that once heralded the start of countless childhood adventures. Now it ushers in a different journey, one I've delayed for far too long. "Just a house," I whisper to myself, but as the musty air hits me, laden with the scent of old books and traces of my father's cologne.

The walls, crammed with dust-coated books and adorned with faded family photos, don't answer. Sun-bleached curtains flutter like spectral hands guiding me into the heart of my past. Everything is untouched, preserved; a museum exhibit of my former life.

"Should have come back sooner," I murmur, my voice swallowed by the silence. My fingertips graze the spines of worn novels on the shelves—each one a world my father had escaped to, away from the clutches of his illness. He's everywhere yet nowhere within these walls.

My gaze falls upon the framed photo beside the couch, our last family picture. We're all smiling—mom, dad, and me, the day of my high school graduation.

A small box catches my eye, tucked away in the corner of the hall closet. Inside, I find fragments of my past: old photos, school reports, handmade birthday cards. They're tokens of love and pride, each one a whisper of 'I remember.' There's a photo of me holding up a trophy, my face beaming. Dad had snapped that picture right after I won the science fair. He always believed in me, even when I didn't.

"Always my champion," I say, my voice catching. The walls seem to hold their breath, absorbing my words, my pain, my longing.

The crunch of tires on gravel startles me, tearing me from my reverie. I glance out the window to see an

SUV pulling into the driveway. My heart hitches as I watch him step out—Grant Evans, the boy who once knew all my secrets, now a man whose life I know nothing about.

Time has sculpted him, the boyish charm giving way to rugged lines and a confidence that suits him. His hair, still tousled, looks like it's been kissed by the mountain winds, and those blue eyes... they could still drown me if I let them.

I take a deep breath, steeling myself for the encounter. It's funny how a place can change so much and yet feel exactly the same. Wildwood Ridge is like that; it's in the scent of pine needles, the whisper of the leaves, the solid earth beneath my feet—it's home.

"Let's do this, Alli," I pep-talk myself, smoothing down my blouse, trying to reclaim some semblance of composure. Opening the door, I step out to meet my past.

"Allison," he grins, his voice is a rich baritone that ripples through the stillness.

For a heartbeat, we're statues in the golden afternoon light, remnants of another time. It's his jaw, sharper now, along with the silver threads catching the light in his hair. He's the same Grant, yet the lines of experience etched into his face speak of untold years lived without me.

"Hey, Grant," I manage, the words tasting strange and formal in my mouth. Does he hear the way my heart stutters, the way it used to whenever he was near?

"Hey." His greeting hangs, suspended between us.

"Been a while," I say, aiming for casual but missing by a mile. Small talk feels clumsy, a poor substitute for the torrent of questions I want to unleash.

"Too long," he agrees, his gaze lingering on my face like a touch. "You look good."

"Thanks." I tuck a strand of auburn hair behind my ear, conscious of his gaze following the movement. "So do you."

"Wildwood Ridge agrees with me," he admits, a half-smile tugging at the corner of his mouth.

"Seems to." I nod, though my throat tightens at the admission. This town, this man—they've shaped each other in ways I can only guess at.

After a long moment of silence, I gesture him forward. "You're the realtor, right?"

"Yeah. Your father left it in his will. Said he wanted someone who knew the beauty of the home to sell it to someone else that would appreciate it." His reply is soft and accommodating as we move inside, side by side but not touching. "Looks just like I remember," he comments, glancing around the room that cradles so many shadows of our past.

"It's like a time capsule," I murmur, and his chuckle, warm and low, wraps around me. "Thank you for handling the sale."

"Of course." Grant's voice is gentle, his smile sincere. "It's what I do."

I nod, trying to ignore the pull in my chest, the longing for more than polite conversation. There's a history here, one that whispers through the creak of floorboards and the sigh of the wind through the pines outside.

"Your dad would be glad you're taking care of things," he says, and that simple sentence breaks through the dam, letting a rush of grief and warmth flood in.

"Thanks, Grant." My voice cracks, and I clear my throat, embarrassed. "He loved this place."

"So did we," he adds quietly, and the 'we' envelops me, a reminder of a time when 'us' was a possibility. Another awkward moment passes in silence before he clears his throat and changes the subject. "Can I help you with anything while I'm here?" Grant asks.

There's a lot to sort through. When mom died, dad never got rid of anything. I have years of memories to go through and decades of happiness to sell, trash, or save. "You don't have to do that. Mom and dad were packrats; you know that."

I turn away, busying myself with a stack of papers atop an old oak desk. But Grant's presence is pervasive, like the scent of pine that seeps into everything here. It's hard to concentrate when every little thing seems to whisper his name.

"Your dad kept everything just so," he comments softly, picking up a faded fishing lure from the desk. "He was a good man. Even if he did have a lot of stuff," Grant winks.

"Hey, remember when we built that fort out back?" he asks, gesturing toward the window overlooking the overgrown backyard.

"How could I forget? We were invincible in that fortress of ours."

"Feels like a lifetime ago," he muses, and I catch the note of wistfulness in his voice, mingling with my own longing for simpler times.

"Remember how we used to argue about pizza toppings?" The words slip out before I can stop them, a playful smirk lifting the corners of my mouth. "Do you still hate pineapple pizza?"

Grant chuckles, the sound rich and unexpected in the quiet room. "Hate's a strong word, but let's just say it's not my first choice."

"Good to know some things never change," I quip, my heart skipping a beat as our eyes meet. His gaze holds mine, and for a split second, time folds upon itself, the years dissolving like mist over the ridge outside.

"Hey Alli," Grant starts, hesitation flickering in his eyes for just a moment. "How about catching up over coffee tomorrow? I'm sure you have a lot to do, but if you have a few minutes," he trails off.

"Sure," I reply, the word feeling like a key turning in a lock. "Coffee sounds good."

"Great." His relief is palpable, and his smile reaches his eyes, igniting them with a hope that reflects my own. "I have a couple of showings in the morning and early afternoon. Would 2 pm work?"

I nod, the corners of my mouth lifting in anticipation. "Two is perfect."

"Then it's a date." The term hangs, tender and tentative, a bridge over years of silence.

And as he leaves, closing the door softly behind him, I'm left with the echo of that word—date—and the fluttering in my chest that suggests this could be the beginning of something beautiful, something like coming home.

2

GRANT

The bell above the door chimes softly as I step into 'Bean There,' the familiar scent of freshly ground coffee enveloping me like a comforting hug. Exposed brick walls, adorn with vibrant local artwork, offering a tribute to Wildwood Ridge's creative pulse. Mismatched chairs and tables lend a casual, lived-in feel to the space. It's a warm sanctuary that carries whispers of countless stories, including my own.

In a cozy corner, sunlight bathes Allison in an ethereal glow, her auburn hair igniting into flames of copper and gold. My feet carry me forward, though my heart hesitates with each step. She looks up, and for a moment, it's like we're seventeen again—before life complicated everything.

"Hey," she greets me, her smile hesitant but genuine.

"Hi." I slide into the chair opposite her. "It's been a while."

We fall into awkward small talk, the kind that feels like dancing around the edge of a cliff. "Remember when Mr. Henderson caught us skipping class to hang out here?" I ask, a chuckle breaking through.

Her laughter joins mine, lighter now, like music. "He was so upset even though he'd called out sick, too. You were trying to explain calculus, and all I cared about was the spring dance."

"Which you looked beautiful at, by the way," I say before I can stop myself. Her cheeks flush, and I'm thrown back to prom night under a sky full of stars, the same blush on her cheeks as we swayed to a slow song. The atmosphere was charged with young love and the promise of forever.

Allison's slender fingers delicately brush against her temple as she tucks the loose strand of hair behind her ear. "Those were simpler times, weren't they?"

The nostalgia in her voice wraps around us, knitting together the years we've spent apart. It feels like a lifetime ago and in some ways, it was. We were different people back then.

"Definitely simpler," I agree, feeling a connection reforming as if time hasn't stretched between us, vast and silent.

Allison's eyes take on a distant, pained look as they drift out the window. Her voice quivers with sadness as she speaks again, her words heavy with emotion. "I've been going through Dad's belongings, trying to make sense of it all. It's... more difficult than I thought it would be."

As I reach across the table to cover her hand with mine, I can feel the warmth radiating from her skin, a comforting and grounding sensation amidst the emotional turmoil. Despite the years apart, the familiarity of her touch brings back memories from our teen years.

A lump forms in my throat and I struggle to swallow past it, forming the words, "I can only imagine," in response.

She meets my eyes, green pools shimmering with unshed tears. "I found his collection of vintage model trains last night. He used to spend hours showing them to me, telling me all about their history." Her voice breaks, and she swallows hard.

I don't know what it's like to lose a loved one, but I imagine it isn't easy. "I can remember him telling me those stories. He thought it would bore me into breaking up with you," I chuckle, thumb stroking the back of her hand gently. "He didn't expect me to be interested, but when he found out I was, I think he liked me a little more."

"Yeah," she breathes out, a tear escaping down her cheek. "I miss him so much. I know I haven't come around, so maybe it doesn't seem like I cared, but I do. I did."

"Hey, look at me," I whisper, waiting until her gaze lifts to mine. "He knew how much you loved him. That's what mattered most."

We sit there, hands linked, the rest of the world fading away. Emotions churn inside me as I see the strong, independent woman who once dreamed of a grand future beyond our town's borders, now vulnerable in the face of her loss. And here I am, still grounded in the place where our roots entwined, holding onto her as if I could take away some of the pain.

"Thank you, Grant," she says, squeezing my hand. Her gratitude is a tangible thing, heavy and warm, filling the air between us.

"Always, Allison. Always."

The warmth of the coffee shop settles around us like a worn-in blanket. And soon, we're talking about everything and nothing. Our lives have changed tremendously since we last saw one another and the nostalgia of Bean There allows us to open up.

Allison became an architect, as she always wanted, and she talks about it like it's the only thing keeping her alive. "Green architecture isn't just about design, Grant. It's about shaping the future," she says, passion lighting up those emerald eyes. "Every building we create at Aegis is a step towards sustainability."

I nod, sipping from the vintage blue enamel mug that has somehow become a shared vessel between us, our fingers brushing fleetingly, sending a jolt through my veins—a quiet reminder of the electricity that once defined us.

"Wildwood Realty's been good to me too." My words feel inadequate compared to her global impact. "We've shaped Wildwood Ridge's landscape, keeping the small-town charm intact while making sure it grows sustainably." I think her desire to go to college and change the world influenced how I turned out. Ten years ago I didn't care about my environmental footprint; now it's something engrained into my everyday thinking.

"Youv'e always been a protector of this place," she murmurs, a corner of her mouth lifting in a smile that doesn't quite reach her eyes.

"Someone has to be," I quip back, but there's truth in my jest. This small town, nestled in the rolling hills and surrounded by lush green forests, has shaped me into the person I am today. The people here are warm and welcoming, their essence imbued with a sense of community and belonging. They know each other's names and stories, and they make sure to take care of their own. This town is more than just a physical place; it's a feeling, an integral part of my identity that I carry with me wherever I may go.

"Remember when we tried to save that old oak tree by the school?" Her laugh is a musical thread weaving through the air, tying a knot around my heart.

"Hard to forget." The memory is vivid: the two of us, young and fired up, chaining ourselves to the ancient trunk, believing we could change the world one tree at a time. The bark was rough under our hands, craggy and weathered from years of standing tall against wind and rain. Our fingers intertwined around each other's as we stood united in our cause. "We thought we were invincible."

"Naïve more like," she counters, but the softness in her gaze tells me she cherishes that memory too.

The conversation ebbs and flows, a dance of words that brings us closer with every step. We talk about our achievements, our setbacks—the daily grind that has filled our lives since we last spoke. But beneath the surface-level exchange, there's an undercurrent of something deeper, a pull towards each other that refuses to be ignored.

"Grant, do you ever think about what we lost?" Her question is a pebble dropped into the still waters of our past, rippling out to touch every hidden crevice.

"Every day," I admit, heart laid bare. "You leaving almost broke me. My mama always said I'd move on, but I still think of you all the time."

"Me too," she confesses, her voice a whisper that seems to echo through the years we've spent apart. "Leaving Wildwood Ridge... leaving you... It was necessary for me to grow," she says softly, her hand creeping across the table toward mine.

"But it hurt." The words tumble out before I can stop them, raw and real.

"More than anything," she agrees, her fingers finally finding mine, twining together like they're meant to be.

In the grip of nostalgia, we sit steeped in the emotions of what was and what might have been. The ache of our breakup, the void it left in both our lives—it's all there in the open now, no longer a silent specter but a bridge reconnecting us.

"Maybe this is our second chance," I venture with a smile, heart thumping against my ribs with the hope of what could lie ahead.

Her smile is hopeful, a promise whispered without words. "Maybe."

The last rays of the day wash the café in a warm, amber glow, casting patterns on the exposed brick walls. The café begins its slow transformation from an oasis of reminiscence to a vessel of quiet goodbyes.

"Would you like to grab dinner with me at The Hidden Table?" I ask, trying to sound casual, but there's a tremor in my words that betrays the gravity of the invitation. "We could... continue catching up?"

Her eyes flicker with uncertainty, and for a moment, I'm back in high school, daring to ask her to prom in a hallway thrumming with teenage angst. "I should really get back to sorting through Dad's things," she says, biting her lip. Her green eyes, still as arresting as the day I first met her, hold a storm of unspoken thoughts.

My heart sinks, and I wonder if it shows on my face —the disappointment, the echo of partings past. I can't help but think of every time I let her slip away before, all because I couldn't find the right words or the courage to speak them. But this time, I watch her closely, searching for some sign of the connection we've rekindled today.

"Of course," I say, my voice quiet. "That's important."

But then, there it is—the flicker across her features, so fleeting I might have missed it if I weren't so attuned to her every expression. It's the same look she'd give when she was about to change her mind about something, a silent conversation we've had a hundred times without speaking a word.

"Actually, my dad's stuff can wait until tomorrow. Dinner sounds wonderful," she says, and the weight lifts off my chest like fog burning away under the morning sun.

"Really?" I can't keep the hope out of my voice, nor do I want to.

"Really," she replies with a soft smile that lights up the dimming café. "The boxes aren't going anywhere."

We get up and head outside, leaving the sanctuary of 'Bean There' behind us. The mountain air is crisp, carrying the scent of pine and the whisper of possibilities. As we walk toward The Hidden Table, I realize that this isn't just about reliving the past or what could have been—it's about what could be.

And as the first stars begin to prick the twilight sky, I'm filled with a sense of hope that burns brighter than any star—hope for renewed love, for healing, for a future where Allison and I don't have to say goodbye again.

3

ALLISON

The Hidden Table is a warm cocoon of light in the cool mountain air. I slide into the booth, my gaze catching on the flickering candles that dot the rustic wooden tables. Grant follows suit, his familiar grin bringing forth a tide of comfort.

The walk from Bean There was perfect. I didn't know if I'd made the right decision until Grant started reminiscing about our high school years.

Now, as we make ourselves comfortable, he remembers the science fair from long ago. "Remember when we thought adding extra baking soda would make our volcano the star of the show?" His chuckle ripples through the intimate space.

"Instead, Mrs. Harmon's wig nearly became a casualty," I laugh, the ruby liquid in my wine glass swaying with my mirth. The memory is vivid, as if the science fair fiasco happened yesterday instead of over a decade ago.

Being with Grant is like coming home after a long day. I can't believe after all this time, we're still so comfortable with one another.

"And we were prom royalty that year," he says, raising his glass in a playful toast. "We peaked early."

I clink my glass against his, the sound crystalline and sweet. "Speak for yourself, Evans. I'm just getting started." But beneath the banter, there's an undercurrent of what might have been. We were so sure of our future, once.

Grant's expression softens; the lines of his face are more defined now, speaking to years of experience I haven't shared. "Would you have stayed, Ali, if things were different?"

The question hangs between us, heavy with implications. A part of me—the part that left this town in search of something bigger—wants to dismiss it, but the truth is more complicated. The nostalgia wraps around us, as tangible as the scent of pine from the surrounding mountains.

"Sometimes, I wonder..." My voice trails off. I ponder what our lives could have looked like, intertwined and steadfast. Would the independence I fought for taste as sweet?

He admits, "Me too," his eyes reflecting the candlelight and something more—a longing that mirrors my own.

My heart beats a rhythm of possibilities. It's a dance we've begun without knowing the steps, one that leads us through the delicate terrain of 'what ifs.' I can almost see the alternate paths, overlaid upon the reality of our separate journeys.

"Would we have been happy?" I muse aloud, the words laced with a vulnerability I rarely allow myself to feel.

"Who knows? But I like to think we would have made a great team, in any life." His smile is soft, thoughtful, and it stirs something within me.

A breeze whispers through the open window, carrying with it the scent of earth and growth. It's a reminder of the ever-present force of nature in Wildwood Ridge—the constant cycle of endings and beginnings. We're a part of that cycle, Grant and I.

"Maybe this is our second season," I say, allowing the idea to bloom amidst the remnants of our laughter and shared memories. There's fear in considering the possibility, but also an undeniable excitement. With Grant across from me, the past feels close enough to touch, yet the future stretches out, inviting and unseen.

"I'd like to think so, Ali. I really would." His voice is a low hum, resonating with the kind of sincerity that has always made him impossible to resist.

I let out a breath I didn't know I was holding, the wine in my glass catching the dim light as I take another sip. The flavors are complex, layered, much like the emotions swirling between us. Tonight, the past isn't a shadow—it's a bridge, and I find myself wanting to cross it, hand in hand with the boy who once knew all my secrets. Now, perhaps, we can share new ones.

Without warning, Grant reaches for my hand. The contact is electric, sending a jolt up my arm. His fingers twine with mine, strong yet impossibly gentle. In that touch, I feel the years peel away, exposing tender wounds and undulled yearnings.

Our gazes lock—a silent conversation where words are needless. It's as if I'm back in high school, under the bleachers, where promises were whispered and futures imagined. But this isn't just nostalgia; it's an acknowledgment of something unfinished, something that still smolders between us, refusing to be extinguished by time or distance.

"Ali," he leans in, his breath warm against my skin, "I've tried, but moving on... it hasn't been easy."

My heart flutters like a trapped bird against its cage. How can a few simple words undo me? Yet they do, unraveling all the carefully placed stitches that held my resolve together. "Grant," I start, but my voice is barely a whisper, "I feel it too."

The admission hangs in the air, fragile and potent. We're standing on a precipice, teetering between what was and what could be. It's terrifying, the way my past collides with the present, threatening to shape an unknown future.

"Sometimes," he continues, his thumb tracing circles on the back of my hand, "I think about how different things would be if you'd stayed. If we'd..."

"Made different choices?" I finish for him, my own thumb mirroring his movements.

"Exactly."

A memory flashes—our fingers laced together as we stood on the edge of Wildwood Ridge lake, the water reflecting the myriad of stars above us, both of us too scared to dive into the unknown depths below.

"Choices brought us back here, didn't they?" I say, trying to steady my racing pulse. It's a question loaded with implications, with the weight of unspoken dreams and muted desires.

In truth, my father's death brought me back here, but even that was a choice. One of many in a long string of decisions that led to this moment.

"Maybe they did." His gaze never wavers, and in those depths, I see the reflection of my own hopes.

We stay like that, hands clasped, souls laid bare, while the rest of the world fades into the periphery. In this moment, there's only Grant and me—the boy who once captured my heart and the man who might never fully release it.

Dinner winds to a close an hour later. After the intimate moment of longing that we shared before the waiter arrived, we settled into a rhythm of conversation that lasted through the appetizer and entree.

I've dated several men since leaving Wildwood Ridge, but I never felt as comfortable as I did with Grant tonight. I missed him, more than I ever really knew. It took coming back to the mountain to realize that I never moved on, not really.

As we rise from the table, Grant's hand leaves mine for a moment. The coldness that replaces his warmth makes me yearn for him even though he's only a few feet away. "Shall we?" He asks, offering his hand once more.

With the promise of the night not yet over, I entangle my fingers in his and let him lead me to the exit.

"Remember when we thought this place was magical?" I say, my voice threading through the silence of

Wildwood Ridge. The streets are empty, shops shut down and families nestled in their homes to enjoy another quiet evening.

"Magic or not," he replies, his gaze following the dance of constellations above us, "I've always found something special here. Especially tonight."

I turn towards him, feeling an audacious spark ignite within me. My heart throbs against my ribcage, each beat a drumroll to the boldness rising in my throat.

"Grant," I begin, steadying my breath as I lock eyes with him, "would you... would you like to continue this walk down memory lane? At my place?"

There's a long pause. He studies my face as if seeking the truth behind my invitation, weighing the gravity of it. His hesitation is palpable, a silent dialogue between caution and desire.

"Are you sure?" he asks, his voice betraying a vulnerability I've not seen before.

"More than ever," I answer, surprised by the certainty in my own words. It's as if all roads have led to this moment, every choice carving out this path back to him.

"Then yes," he says, his affirmation sending a surge of relief and excitement coursing through me. "Yes, I'd like that."

Our hands find each other once again, fingers lacing with a sense of purpose. As we walk, the memories flood in—lazy summer days by the lake, the thrill of stolen kisses under cover of darkness, the bitter-sweet goodbye at the crossroads of our futures. Each flashback is a tender bruise on my soul, colored with what was lost and what might be regained.

The chill of the evening wraps around us, but his touch is a firebrand against the cold. Our inter-twined hands are a bridge across the years we spent apart, a silent vow to explore the possibilities that time has kept at bay.

"Tonight feels like a beginning, doesn't it?" I whisper, more to myself than to him.

"It does," he agrees, his thumb caressing my skin in a way that speaks louder than words.

Grant drives me home. An old Kenny Chesney song plays on the radio as he asks if I'd feel more comfort-able at his place. "You know," he blushes, "if being around all your father's stuff is too much."

My home isn't far from downtown Wildwood ridge and as we draw near, the soft glow from the windows bids us welcome. This threshold, like so many others we've crossed tonight, holds the potential of new memories, of second chances. With each step closer, I feel the potent blend of past and present weaving into the fabric of a future neither of us dared to dream until now.

"My place is fine." We shared so many memories within these walls. "Let's see where this goes," I say, my voice steady despite the whirlwind inside me.

"Let's," he echoes, and the hope in his eyes mirrors my own.

4

GRANT

I lead Allison along the path where we once raced as kids, a narrow gravel ribbon that snakes its way through the tall pines of Wildwood Ridge. There's a rhythm to our footfalls, a syncopated dance of boots against stone and earth that pulls at the chords of my memory. The air is tinged with pine, cool and crisp, and I swear it's laced with something more potent than oxygen—something that quickens my pulse and stirs a warmth in my core.

"Remember when we used to think these woods were enchanted?" Allison's voice is soft but clear, carried on the mountain breeze.

"Of course. We were adventurers, conquerors of realms," I reply, smiling at the thought. "Seems like a lifetime ago."

With each step, echoes of laughter and whispered promises resurface, and I can't help but feel both the comfort of what was and the ache of what could have been.

"Everything feels so small now... yet so vast," she muses, her gaze taking in the expanse of trees and sky.

"Perspective changes everything," I say, though I'm not just talking about the landscape.

At the threshold of her childhood home, Allison pauses, her fingertips caressing the doorknob, weathered and familiar. It's as if time has thinned here, the barrier between then and now reduced to the gossamer veil of memory. The sound of our shared past seems to thrum behind the door, a symphony of joy and sorrow.

"Are you okay?" I ask, resting my hand on her shoulder, feeling the tension knotted beneath my palm.

"More than okay," she responds, though her voice wavers ever so slightly. "It's just... overwhelming.

Not that you being here is overwhelming," Allison begins to talk faster. "Just that the last time we were really here together, our lives were totally different. And I don't know what I'm nervous about, but I'm nervous." She ends with an anxious laugh.

"Take all the time you need. I'm right here," I assure her, and I mean it in more ways than one.

"Grant..." Her voice trails off, and she leans back into my touch, her body language confessing things unsaid. "Thank you for being here."

"Always." The words slip out, heavy with emotion and truth. "There's no place I'd rather be."

As she turns the knob and pushes the door open, a ghostly rush of warmth spills out, wrapping around us like an old blanket. I feel her shiver, though I'm not sure if it's from the cool mountain air or the surge of memories flooding through the opened doorway.

"Let's go in," I suggest, squeezing her shoulder gently. "Together."

We cross the threshold side by side, the past reaching out to greet us with open arms. And as the door swings shut behind us, sealing us in this intimate cocoon of history and longing, I realize that this isn't just a homecoming—it's a new beginning. A second chance.

The door to Allison's childhood room creaks open from the wind barreling through the front door, and we're greeted by a faded yellow that once shimmered like sunshine. I close the door behind me and follow her. She walks to her room with purpose.

The air is thick with the scent of dust and memories, and I watch as her eyes dance over every little artifact of her past.

"It's like stepping back in time."

"Your mixtapes," I point out, picking up one from the stack on her dresser. It's labeled in her scribbled handwriting: 'Summer Jams '08.' A smile tugs at my lips. "Remember when we thought these would be worth something someday?"

Allison laughs, a sound that ripples through me. "We were such dreamers."

"Still are," I murmur, meeting her gaze. The air between us feels charged, alive with old sparks that refuse to die.

Her fingers brush over the spines of books lined up like soldiers on a shelf. Each title is a marker of days when all we had was time and each other. She pulls one out, its pages worn from countless reads, and our hands touch. My heart stutters at the contact, familiar yet new.

"Look," she says, holding up the book to show a passage marked with a folded corner. "This is the one I read aloud to you that night on the porch swing."

"Under the stars," I add, remembering the sound of her voice mixing with the chorus of crickets. "I think that was the moment I knew I would never get over you."

"Grant..." Her voice trails off, and there's a softness in her eyes that makes me feel both exposed and sheltered.

I reach for another book, opening it to a random page. "And you fell asleep while I was reading this one to you." The memory of her head on my shoulder, her breaths deep and even, floods through me.

"Because I felt safe with you," she admits, and my chest tightens.

We move to sit on the edge of her bed, the mattress groaning under our weight as if in protest of the years gone by. Above us, the walls are a collage of who we used to be—posters of bands we swore would change the world, stickers that once held the promise of forever.

"Remember our first time?" Her question comes softly, almost hesitant, and I turn to face her.

"Here?" I ask, though I know exactly what she means. My pulse quickens.

She nods. "It was...awkward."

"Exhilarating," I correct her, and we both chuckle. "We were so nervous."

"I thought my heart was going to beat out of my chest," she confesses, and I reach out to tuck a strand of auburn hair behind her ear.

"Mine too," I say, letting my fingers linger against her skin.

The room seems to shrink, the distance between us filled with an electric current. My thumb brushes her jawline, and I'm transported back to those feverish moments of discovery over a decade ago.

"Everything changed after that night," she whispers, leaning into my touch.

"Changed for the better," I affirm, my voice steady even as my insides quake.

Her hand finds mine, and we're intertwined, the threads of our past weaving a complex tapestry. There's a magnetism here, in the place where our journey began, pulling us together with the promise of what could be.

"Grant," she says, her voice laced with something unspoken, "do you ever think about how different things could've been?"

"Every day," I admit, tracing circles on the back of her hand. "But we're here now, Allison. That's what matters."

The glow from the star-shaped stickers casts a celestial light over us, and I can't help but feel that maybe, just maybe, the universe has aligned for this exact moment. For us.

"Being with you again," she starts, then stops. Her green eyes search mine, looking for reassurance, for hope.

"Feels like coming home," I finish for her, and it's true. With Allison, I am home.

"Shh," I whisper, tracing the line of her jaw, feeling her pulse quicken under my touch. "Let me just... look at you."

She leans into me, those emerald eyes holding mine, and there's an entire conversation in that gaze—questions and answers, fears and assurances, all swirling together in silent communion. My heart expands, threatening to burst from the sheer intensity of emotion.

"Remember how we used to talk about traveling the world?" she murmurs, her breath warm against my lips.

"Every star up there was a dream we had," I reply, each word laced with the taste of nostalgia. "But right now, you're every dream come to life."

Our lips meet, and it's like the first drop of rain after a parching drought. The sweetness of her mouth is a memory reborn, a connection reignited, stirring sensations that lay dormant for far too long. I kiss her deeper, the hunger for her eclipsing everything else, our past melding into the present.

"God, Allison," I groan against her lips, "I've missed this... missed you."

"Me too," she breathes, her hands finding their way to my hair, pulling me closer.

In this room where we first discovered each other years before, we discover each other again by stripping down. I start with the buttons of her blouse, each one slipping free, revealing more of the woman whose absence marked me indelibly. She assists, her nimble fingers working on my shirt, her touch igniting trails of fire along my skin.

"Each piece," she says softly, her eyes locked on mine as my shirt falls away, "is like letting go of the what-ifs, isn't it?"

"Letting go, or maybe... reclaiming what should've been ours all along." My voice is thick with emotion as I help slide her blouse off her shoulders, the fabric whispering to the floor.

Her hands shake slightly as she undoes my belt, but there's conviction in her movements, a determination that mirrors my own. We discard our past layer by layer, not rushing despite the urgency pulsing through us—the need to relearn each other, to explore both the familiar and the uncharted territories of our bodies and hearts.

As the last barriers fall away, leaving us vulnerable and exposed, I'm struck by the raw beauty of this moment. Here, among the keepsakes of our youth and beneath the ghostly glow of stars, we stand ready to forge new memories, to heal old wounds with the balm of our passion.

"Grant," she whispers, cupping my face, "let's make this night ours."

"Always," I vow, knowing that this time, nothing will pull us apart.

5

ALLISON

My skin shivers under Grant's touch as his fingers trace the familiar lines of my body, a map he once knew by heart. His delicate kisses fall like the first snowflakes of Wildwood Ridge's early winters—soft, gentle, and full of promise. "I've missed you," I whisper into the charged air, my voice laced with vulnerability.

"I've missed you, too. Every day, Allison," he breathes against my neck, sending a cascade of goosebumps down my spine. "Every single day."

His hands are a melody across my flesh, playing every chord of longing and desire that's been silently building between us since our eyes met again in this small town all those years ago. As he explores, each caress is a word unsaid, a memory relived. The warmth of his mouth travels the expanse of my torso, igniting fires in places that had grown cold since his departure from my life.

"Grant..." My back arches as he descends, kissing his way to the center of my pleasure. It's an intimacy so raw, so exposing, that it feels like coming home. He parts me with reverence, his tongue writing sonnets on my sensitive folds as I tangle my fingers in his hair, anchoring myself in the here and now.

"Ah, God... Yes..." My voice breaks on the cresting waves of ecstasy, the mounting pressure in the pit of my stomach a testament to his skillful devotion.

His hands roam across my stomach as he drags his tongue relentlessly over my clit. His beard brushes against my sensitive flesh, sending shivers up and down my spine.

Moaning softly into the rhythm of his tongue's movements, I wrap my legs around his head. He takes it as an invitation to thrust two fingers inside me, slowly stretching me open.

I gasp at the sensation, feeling both full and wanting more at the same time. The bed groans beneath us as I dig my nails into his shoulders. Grant works his fingers in a faster cadence, as if reading the tempo of my breaths to give me what I need.

"Grant..." He continues to tease and probe at my bundle of nerves, enjoying the feeling of me writhing beneath him.

Suddenly, I feel a coil tighten in the pit of my stomach. Pleasure courses through my veins as his fingers hit my G-spot with unerring accuracy. His mouth continues to suckle and lap at my clit, pushing me closer to the edge. And then suddenly release washes over me in a shatter climax, leaving me breathless and sweaty.

Grant carefully shifts above me, our gazes locked—a silent conversation of what we are and what we could be. His eyes, so blue and deep, hold stories of the years we spent apart, yet they also glimmer with the hope of a future we might reclaim.

As he invades my core, the fiery intimacy burns wildly, consuming my very essence. "I feel you," I whisper, my voice barely a husky sigh. "Every inch of you."

Grant's reply is a raw promise, his rhythmic thrusts a passionate declaration, laying claim to the depths within me anew.

Each powerful thrust is a carnal plea for forgiveness, every lusty moan an explicit note in our symphony of redemption. We weave our bodies together, finding an intoxicating rhythm that belongs only to us—a sensual cadence that pulsates with the promise of second chances and naughty beginnings. My heart throbs, thumping in sync with our raw union, as if it knows this is the sinfully sweet spot it's destined to be.

Our hungry gazes lock, bodies magnetized by an undeniable chemistry. He's all muscle and desire, every tendon flexed in testament to his primal need for me.

I trail my fingertips across his biceps, caressing the hills and valleys of his body. Grant grabs my ass and plunges into me over and over again with lust-soaked passion, leaving us both gasping.

The world outside the window fades to a blur of moonlit shadows as Grant and I find our rhythm.

"Grant," I breathe out his name like a sacred incantation, my voice laced with the weight of every moment we've lost and found again.

"Allison," he whispers back, each syllable a stroke against my heart as his hands roam over me. His touch is both familiar and thrillingly new, rediscovering territories once mapped but never forgotten.

Our bodies move with a shared urgency, a silent acknowledgment of the time we've spent apart. It's a crescendo of skin on skin, an intimate ballet that propels us toward the edge of reason. The mountainous backdrop seems to echo our passion, its untamed beauty resonating with our own wild abandon.

"Look at me," Grant urges gently, and I lift my gaze to meet his. In his eyes, I see the reflection of my own soul—a mix of vulnerability and strength. He sees me, truly sees me, beyond the facade I present to the rest of the world.

"Remember us," he says, and it's not a command, but a plea—one that I answer with every fiber of my being. I remember the innocence of first love, the sting of goodbye, and the serendipity of this second chance.

"Yes," I reply, my voice a whisper against the symphony of our union.

As we reach the pinnacle of our desire, a climax washes over us like a cleansing rain. It's powerful and pure, leaving us breathlessly intertwined, a tangle of limbs and fulfilled yearnings.

In the stillness that follows, I lie there, wrapped in the warmth of Grant's embrace. The echoes of our pleasure linger in the room, a sensual sonnet that continues to play softly in the background.

I close my eyes, and my mind drifts to all the choices that have led me here—to this man, to this town, to the healing of old wounds. I think of the ambitions that drove me away from Wildwood Ridge, the relentless pursuit of success, the ache of losing my father. And now, lying beside the man who has been the silent guardian of my heart's memories, I'm struck by life's unpredictable currents.

"Thank you, Grant," I murmur into the darkness, my gratitude for this night, for his patience, for the forgiveness that we've granted each other, spilling forth without restraint.

"For what?" His voice is soft, a gentle rumble that vibrates against my skin.

"For waiting. For believing. For tonight." My words are a bare whisper, laden with the weight of my emotions.

"Always," he promises, a vow that encompasses more than just this night—it stretches into the days and years ahead.

As my mind wanders through the tapestry of my past, I realize that Grant has reignited something within me that I thought was lost forever—the ember of love that burns brightly, undiminished by time or distance. My journey, fraught with its trials and triumphs, has led me back to him, back home.

And in the quiet sanctuary of Grant's arms, under the vast expanse of the star-studded sky, I understand that sometimes the greatest strength lies in surrendering to the pull of the heart—a lesson learned among the mountains of Wildwood Ridge.

6

ALLISON

The morning sun slips through the half-open blinds, its tendrils of light unfurling across my childhood bedroom. Golden hues dance over the faded ballerina wall hangings, and I awaken slowly, savoring the dreamy residue of last night's intimacy with Grant. The taste of his kiss lingers on my lips like the sweetest honey, and I let out a soft sigh of delight.

I'm cocooned in the old twin bed that knows all my secrets, its familiar yet faded cotton sheets a testament to years gone by. I stretch languidly, feeling every fiber of my being still humming from Grant's touch. My hand drifts to the edge of the mattress, fingers tracing the worn fabric of Binky, my child-hood teddy bear. His one eye is hanging by a thread, but he's still my silent confidant.

"Remember when life was just skinned knees and starry-eyed dreams, Binky?" I murmur to the tattered bear. The room is quiet, save for the gentle whisper of leaves rustling outside my window.

I reflect on the unexpected events—the desperate phone call from father's neighbor, saying he had a heart attack—that brought me back to Wildwood Ridge, a place I had packed away along with Binky and my ballet slippers.

"Did I ever imagine I'd come back here?" My thoughts are a tangled web as I try to reconcile the ambitious woman I've become with the girl who once believed this small town was her entire universe. I consider the impact of my return, not just the healing after Dad's passing, but what it means for me... for us...

"Grant," I breathe out, the name stirring a kaleido-scope of emotions inside me. He's the same, yet different—more rugged, more earnest. The way he looked at me last night, it was as if we were teenagers again, stealing moments beneath the sheltering pines.

I take a deep breath, each inhale bringing clarity, each exhale releasing the past. There's a sense of hope budding within me, fragile but determined, much like the first spring blooms pushing through thawing earth outside.

"Wildwood Ridge," I say, letting the words hang in the air, imbued with nostalgia and possibility. Here, amidst the mountains and memories, maybe Grant and I can unearth the remnants of a love that never truly faded.

"Is it foolish to believe we can heal?" I ask the empty room, though I'm really asking myself. But there's no answer, only the warm embrace of the morning sun nudging me towards the day ahead—a day that could mark the beginning of everything.

The creak of the old wooden door jolts me from my reverie, and I watch as morning light spills around Grant's silhouette. He steps into the room, his presence enveloping the space like a melody long forgotten, yet somehow imprinted in the soul.

"Good morning," he says, every syllable tinged with a hope so bright it rivals the sun's caress on the wall hangings of my childhood. He pads across the room, each step deliberate, closing the distance between us. "Allison, I've been thinking," he starts, his words not just spoken but felt—a vibration through the air that resonates deep within me. "About us, about all those years we lost... I believe in second chances."

I sit up, tucking my legs beneath me on the bedspread that Grandma sewn, its threads holding decades of whispered secrets and silent wishes. Grant's optimism unfurls in the room, wrapping around my guarded heart with a warmth that feels both terrifying and comforting.

"Can we really start over?" I ask, the skepticism in my voice softened by the longing in my eyes.

His hand reaches out, hesitates for the briefest moment—an eternity wrapped in a second—before finding mine. His touch is familiar, grounding, like the soft hum of crickets that used to serenade us during those endless mountain summers. It's a touch that speaks of forgiveness, of healing, and I can't help but cling to it like a lifeline.

"Look at me, Allison." His voice is gentle, coaxing.

I lift my gaze, letting it wander from the golden hues cast by the sun to settle into the depths of his blue eyes. They are oceans of sincerity, and love crashes over me in waves. I'm drowning in the raw emotion that flickers there—a kaleidoscope of desire, regret, and unwavering affection.

"Grant..." I whisper his name like a prayer, or perhaps a curse. The weight of our past, the depth of our connection—it's all too much and not enough at the same time.

"We're not the same people we were," he continues, his thumb tracing circles over the back of my hand, sending ripples of sensation through my skin. "But I think that's a good thing. We've grown, learned... Surely that counts for something?"

"Doesn't it scare you?" My voice cracks with vulnerability. "The possibility that we might repeat the same mistakes?" That I might repeat the same mistakes... that I might leave him again.

"Terrifies me," he admits without hesitation. "But what scares me more is never knowing what could have been if we don't try. I have loved you my entire life, Allison."

There's an honesty to Grant's words that strips away the layers of hurt and doubt that have cocooned me for years.

"Ally," he begins, his voice a gentle rumble that reverberates through the silence, stirring old yearnings within my chest. "I have to ask—would you consider giving us another chance? Here, in Wildwood Ridge?"

The words hang suspended in the sun-drenched air, motes of dust swirling around them like tiny planets orbiting a newfound sun. Each syllable is laden with the kind of hope that feels too fragile to hold, fear that threatens to shatter it, and a longing so acute it could carve canyons in my heart.

I draw in a ragged breath, searching for the courage that seems to come so easily to him. My mind teeters on the edge of the precipice between past and present, memories cascading like a waterfall. The town fair, where laughter danced on the breeze; the woods, where the earthy scent of pine filled our lungs as we hiked trails worn by our own footsteps; and those clandestine, starlit kisses that tasted of promise and wild freedom.

"Grant, I—" My voice falters, caught in the thicket of emotion. Old scars itch with the possibility of healing, of rewriting endings into beginnings. "I'm scared," I confess, the vulnerability in my admission knitting the space between us tighter.

"Me too," he says, his thumb tracing circles on the back of my hand. "But if we let fear decide for us, we'll never know what we could've had."

His touch is an anchor in the tumultuous sea of my thoughts. I look at him, really look, and see not just the boy I once loved, but the man before me—willing to stand amidst the wreckage of our past and build something new.

"Wildwood Ridge," I murmur, rolling the words around in my mouth like a fine wine. It's more than just a place—it's where my father's laughter still echoes in the wind, where every corner holds a story, where Grant's love, once tender and tentative, has grown roots waiting to be unearthed.

"Wildwood Ridge," Grant repeats, his blue eyes reflecting the earnest sky outside.

And in those eyes, I find the map to a treasure I didn't realize I'd been seeking. Home isn't just where you lay your head—it's where you anchor your heart. And mine...mine is tethered to this town, to the memories, to the man whose hands are calloused from holding onto hope.

"Let's take that chance," I whisper, the decision settling over me like the first snowfall—quiet, transformative, inevitable.

Our fingers entwine, a silent vow cast in flesh and bone. Grant's smile is a sunrise that promises warmth after the longest night, and I bask in its glow, feeling the thaw of a winter I spent away from here, from him.

"Then it's a new beginning," he says, pulling me closer until our foreheads touch, sharing breath, sharing this sliver of time that feels endless. His heartbeat against my chest is steady and sure, a drumbeat calling me back to life.

"Let's do it right this time," I say against his neck, inhaling the scent of pine and earth that clings to him, the essence of Wildwood Ridge itself.

"Let's make new memories," he whispers back, his breath warm on my skin. "Together."

Our embrace deepens, his hands tracing the contours of my back as if memorizing the map of my body anew. In his touch, there's healing; in his kiss, redemption. And in his eyes, I see our shared history and the unwritten chapters of our story stretching out before us—filled with hope, forgiveness, and second chances.

For more books...

Check out my website:

https://geni.us/KelsieCalloway

HAVE YOU LEFT A REVIEW?

Reviews are an author's bread and butter. This is how new readers find us and how old readers determine if a new series is worth their time. If you enjoyed this book, take a moment to leave a review or put in a recommendation on BookBub.

Scan with your phone camera!